To Benjamin

From......................

It was Christmas Eve and Benjamin was snug and warm in his cozy bed. He was trying so hard to go to sleep. But he could hear strange noises.

It wasn't the sound of sleigh bells.
It wasn't the sound of reindeer hoofs on the roof.
It wasn't even the sound of Santa unpacking his sack.

It was more of a

HARUMPH!

and an

OOF!

It was no use.

There'd be no sleep for Benjamin
until he'd found out what
was making that noise.

Benjamin crept down the stairs
and peered into the living room.
There were three stockings
hanging from the fireplace.

One of them belonged to Benjamin. But where had the other two come from? Suddenly, a muffled voice came from the chimney.

"Oh, dear. I'm even **more** stuck now!"

There was a scuffling sound from behind the Christmas tree, and Benjamin jumped as a small elf appeared.

"Uh, hello," said the elf. "I guess you've caught us!"

Benjamin listened as the elf explained
that Santa was stuck in the chimney.
The elf had tried to pull him out. But the
only things that had come down so far
were Santa's boots and pants!

"I can help you," suggested Benjamin. "I'll hold Santa's feet and we can both pull." The elf agreed. "Between us, we might be able to get him unstuck."

Benjamin grasped both of Santa's feet firmly.
But, just at that moment, a light went on upstairs.
"Benjamin, is that you?" called his mom. "Back to
bed now, please, or Santa won't come!"

At that exact moment,
Santa shot back up
the chimney... with
Benjamin still hanging
onto his feet.

The poor elf could not believe his eyes.
But there was no time to think...
Benjamin's mom was coming
out of her bedroom.

"I'm coming!" squeaked the elf. He hurried
up the stairs and jumped into Benjamin's
bed, pulling the covers up over his head.
"Night-night, sweetie!" said Benjamin's
mom through the doorway.

Meanwhile, up on the roof, Santa and Benjamin had landed in a heap. The clever reindeer had hooked their reins under Santa's arms and pulled as hard as they could.

"Good job!" said Santa, brushing himself down. "No more cookies for me tonight!"

Benjamin scrambled to his feet. But Santa
was so busy, he didn't notice that Benjamin
and the elf had traded places!

"I think we'd better deliver the rest of the
presents first," said Santa, "and leave this
house for last."

Santa climbed into the driver's seat.

"Elf, you get the presents ready for our next destination," he called over his shoulder.
"But I'm not Elf..." replied Benjamin.

Santa wasn't really listening.
He was talking to the reindeer.
"Up, up, and away!" Santa called,
and the reindeer took off before
Benjamin had time to explain.

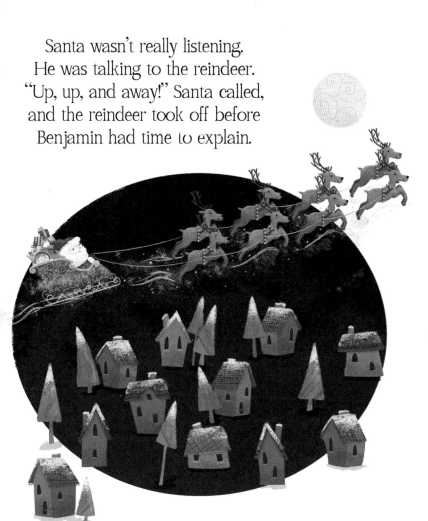

Benjamin held on tight as the
sleigh climbed high into the
night sky, above the rooftops.

Surrounded by sacks, Benjamin was so
busy figuring out which presents were
which, there was no time to let Santa
know that there'd been a mistake.

There were **big**
presents for the cities,

and **SHINY** presents
for the towns.

There were **ODD**-shaped
presents for the villages,

and **mystery**
presents for the farms.

To Benjamin

As they landed at their next stop, Santa decided that he couldn't risk getting stuck in a chimney again.

"Elf, I think you'd better make the deliveries from now on," decided Santa, "while I sort the presents."

Benjamin *shimmied* down chimneys.

He SQUEEZED through cat flaps.

And, if all else failed, he used Santa's *magic* key to let himself in.

In each house, Benjamin picked up the cookies to take home to Mrs. Claus, and carrots for the reindeer.

Finally, there was just one sack left, and
Santa still hadn't realized his mistake!
The sleigh headed back over the
rooftops to Benjamin's house.

To
Benjamin

Benjamin had never had so much
fun as when he slid down his
own chimney with a sack of
his own presents.

He put his presents under the
Christmas tree, then picked up
Santa's pants and boots and
put them in the sack.

"Psst! Elf, where are you?" whispered Benjamin.

A very happy Elf appeared, rubbing his eyes.
"I've had such a lovely nap," he said.
Benjamin handed over the
sack and waved as Elf
disappeared up
the chimney.

Back in his cozy bed, Benjamin listened to the sounds of reindeer hoofs on the roof, sleigh bells, and, very faintly,

"Ho ho ho!

Merry Christmas!"

Or was that,

"Ho ho ho!
yummy cookies!"?

Write your name on the gift tags.

Draw yourself as an elf.

Create one-of-a-kind books for any child on Put Me In The Story!

visit ⟶ www.putmeinthestory.com/morenames

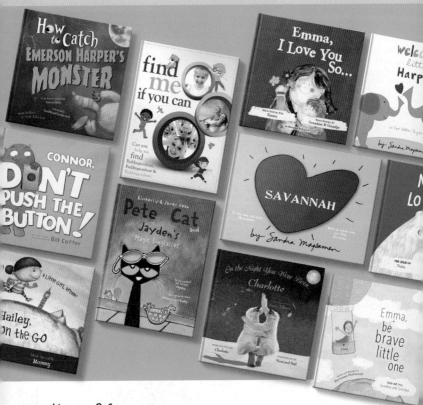